Submarines

Christopher Maynard

Kingfisher

NEW YORK

Contents

Under the sea

B y holding their breath, people can dive down into the sea — but only for a short while. No one can hold their breath long enough to explore something the size of an ocean.

Before diving suits and submarines, we knew next to nothing about the underwater world. Today, though, scientists can dive right down to explore the cold dark waters of the ocean floor.

Diving down

Like all boats, submarines float if left to themselves. They have to put on weight in order to sink under the waves. Submarines have ballast tanks to help them do this.

When its ballast tanks are full of air, a submarine is light enough to float. Letting water into the tanks makes the submarine heavier. Now it can dive deep below the water's surface.

① A submarine has to flood its ballast tanks to make itself heavy enough to dive.

② The submarine sinks when the tanks are full. Stubby wings called diving planes point the boat up or down.

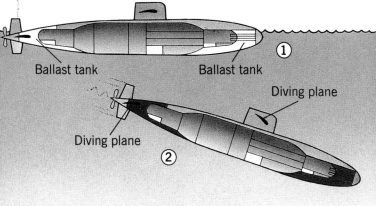

Ballast tank

Ballast tank

①

Diving plane

Diving plane

②

AIR AND WATER

Find out how air can lift things in water. Partly blow up a balloon and knot its neck. Then tie a 10-oz. ball of modeling clay to the balloon. Now drop the balloon into water — it should float. Add more clay to find how much the balloon is able to support.

Balloon half full of air

String

Modeling clay

③ Using up fuel, food, drinking water, and weapons makes the submarine lighter. Trimming tanks are flooded to add weight.

④ The submarine has to be lighter before it can rise. It loses weight by forcing air into the tanks, and driving out the water.

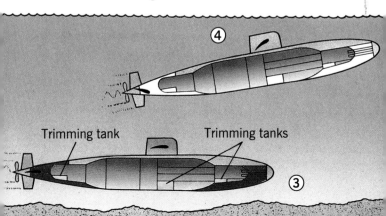

④

Trimming tank

Trimming tanks

③

Bathtub sub

Here's how to build your own model submarine from an empty plastic bottle. Make three holes in the bottle like the ones shown right. Then tape a few heavy coins on either side of the holes. Push a plastic straw over the nozzle of the bottle and seal the joint with modeling clay. Lastly, tape some plastic tubing to the end of the straw.

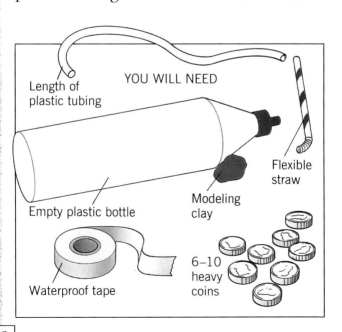

Length of plastic tubing

YOU WILL NEED

Flexible straw

Modeling clay

Empty plastic bottle

Waterproof tape

6–10 heavy coins

8

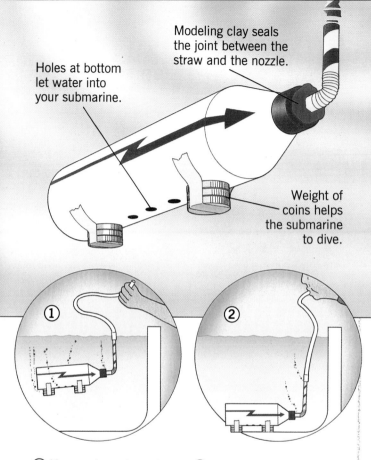

Modeling clay seals the joint between the straw and the nozzle.

Holes at bottom let water into your submarine.

Weight of coins helps the submarine to dive.

① Your submarine will start to sink as water pours in through the holes in the bottom. (Make sure the end of the plastic tubing is out of the water as the submarine dives.)

② Blow into the plastic tubing to push out the water and fill your bath-tub submarine with air. Air is lighter than water, so as the water is forced out, your submarine will start to rise.

Early submarines

Submarines have only become really useful since the early 1900s. People experimented with all kinds of different submarine designs before that, but few of these ideas were a great success at moving around under water.

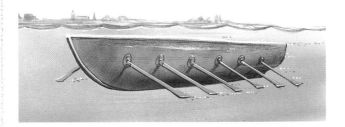

△ An idea tried out in the 1620s was a weighted and covered rowboat.

▷ In 1776, the *Turtle* was the first submarine to be used in war. There was just room for one person inside.

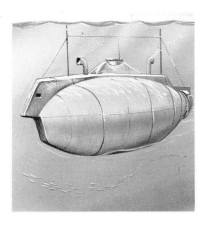

◁ In 1900 the first modern sub, the *Holland*, was bought by the U.S. Navy.

▽ The *Gymnote* was French. In 1906, gas from batteries for its electric motors caught fire.

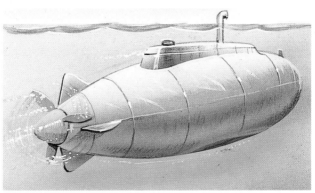

In World War I, submarines were known as "pig boats" in the U.S. Navy. This wasn't because there weren't any showers and the cramped living space made them smelly — they were actually named after porpoises, or "sea pigs!"

Fighting submarines

In both world wars, submarines sank thousands of ships by firing torpedoes at them. Submarines often attacked from beneath the waves, but whenever possible they stayed on the surface where they could move fastest.

A seaplane surprises a World War II German submarine cruising on the surface.

HIDE AND SEEK

Today's submarines can stay underwater for weeks. They find their way around the ocean with special computers called navigation computers. These tell the crew exactly where they are, minute by minute.

Submarines can also listen out for ships and other submarines. They carry equipment called sonar. This lets them pick up the faint sounds of another submarine's engines, or of a ship on the surface, even though the other vessel may be a long way away.

△ Anti-submarine ships use sonar to send out pings of sound. When these hit something, an echo bounces back. By timing how long the echoes take to do this, the ship's crew can tell where the submarine is.

▽ Submarines use sonar equipment to listen for the noise made by enemy ships and submarines.

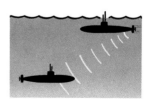

Undersea giants

Modern submarines are very big and fast boats indeed — some are almost the size of ocean liners.

All submarines now have either diesel or nuclear engines. Nuclear submarines no longer have to come to the surface regularly to let in fresh air and recharge their batteries. At sea, they spend a lot of time deep under the waves where the water is calm and quiet.

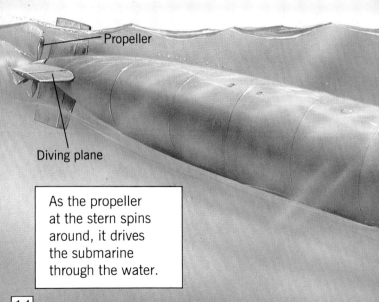

Propeller

Diving plane

As the propeller at the stern spins around, it drives the submarine through the water.

BIG SAIL

The tall tower on the top of a submarine is called a sail. When leaving a harbor, the captain commands the boat from here — it's high up, and it gives the captain good all round views of any other shipping traffic.

Sail

Diving plane

The diving planes move to angle the submarine up or down, or to keep it level. When the submarine isn't too deep in the water, periscopes can be raised to look out over the surface.

A look inside

The heart of a submarine is the control room. It is from here that the captain leads the crew and directs the boat's operations.

Modern submarines usually have two hulls. The inner one is very strong so the boat can dive deep. The outer hull is smooth and streamlined so the boat can slip easily through the water.

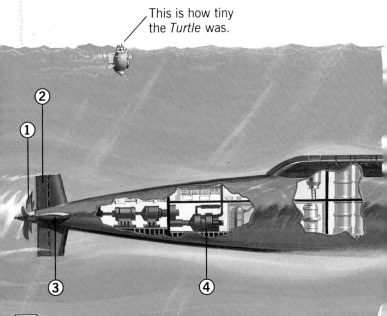

This is how tiny the *Turtle* was.

① ② ③ ④

THE PARTS OF A SUBMARINE

① The propeller drives the boat.
② The rudder steers.
③ The diving planes control angle and depth.
④ The engine.
⑤ A missile is being test-fired.
⑥ A periscope allows the crew to look above the surface.

⑦ The sail holds the periscopes, as well as masts with radio and radar antennas inside them.
⑧ The crew's living quarters.
⑨ Inner hull.
⑩ Outer hull.
⑪ Control room.
⑫ Navigation area.
⑬ Torpedoes.

On patrol

A big submarine may spend ten weeks or more underwater, on patrol at sea. During this time, crew members are kept busy making sure everything runs smoothly. They often take part in battle exercises to practice their skills at handling the submarine in dangerous situations. Life is crowded on board, but still fairly comfortable.

▽ If the submarine is just below the surface, an officer can put up the periscope to see outside.

There is always a team on duty here in the heart of the boat — the control room.

△ The engine room is always located in the stern of the submarine.

▷ In the galley, meals are prepared by a team of cooks. All the ovens are electric, so they don't give off gas fumes. This would be particularly dangerous in such a small area.

▷ Sleeping quarters are small. Officers share cabins, but the rest of the crew members have curtained-off bunks.

Deepsea rescue

I f a submarine gets into trouble and sinks in water that isn't too deep, the crew may be able to escape from it using special waterproof suits. But if the boat is lying too far down, a small deep-diving rescue submarine must be used to bring the crew back to safety on the surface.

▽ Imagine this scene. A crippled submarine is stranded 4,000 feet down, on the ocean floor. It sends up a floating radio and the emergency signals are soon heard.

◁ The operation starts when a small deep-diving rescue vessel is loaded on to an aircraft. It is flown as near as possible to the sunken submarine.

▽ The rescue vessel is taken on a submarine to the accident site.

▷ The rescue vessel dives deep and locks on to the escape hatch of the stranded submarine. Twenty-four crew members scramble into the rescue vessel and are ferried to safety. Several trips have to be made to take off the entire crew.

Very deep dives

All kinds of deepsea craft are used by scientists to study the oceans. Most are tiny, and can carry teams of no more than three or four people. But these craft can dive down thousands of feet. In January 1960, the *Trieste* took three scientists down into the deepest place on Earth, a 7-mile-deep trench in the Pacific Ocean.

WATER PRESSURE

Water is heavy. The deeper you go in it, the more its weight squeezes you. Here is how to feel this water pressure for yourself. Put your hand into a small plastic bag and plunge it into a deep bucket of water — the pressure will force out the air and make the bag squash against your skin.

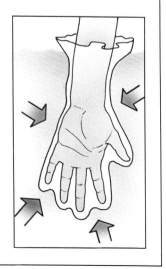

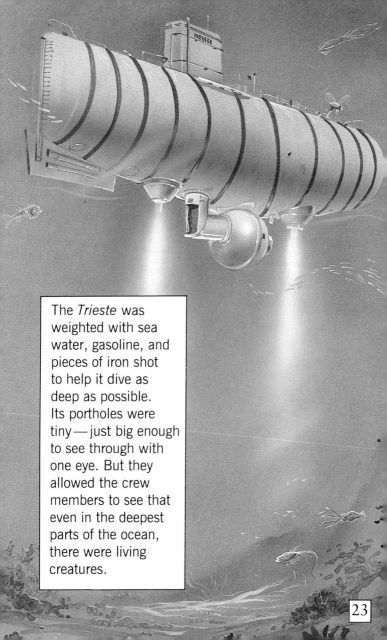

The *Trieste* was weighted with sea water, gasoline, and pieces of iron shot to help it dive as deep as possible. Its portholes were tiny — just big enough to see through with one eye. But they allowed the crew members to see that even in the deepest parts of the ocean, there were living creatures.

23

Discovering wrecks

In the summer of 1985, scientists scanning the seabed discovered the broken wreck of the passenger ship *Titanic*. The ship had been holed by an iceberg in the North Atlantic 73 years earlier. It sank swiftly, and over 1,500 people died. In 1986, the mini-sub *Alvin* used a small robot to explore the wreck.

HOW DARK IS THE SEA?

Sunlight can only warm the top layers of the ocean. As you go deeper, farther away from the Sun's light and heat, the water gets darker and colder. At the bottom it is just a few degrees above freezing.

① Most animals and plants live near the surface, in the sunlit zone.

② The twilight zone is too dark for seaweed and other plants. A few air-breathing animals swim here.

③ The sunless zone is pitch black and icy cold. Only deepsea creatures live here. Some make their own light to lure prey. Other bottom-livers feed on the snowfall of food that drifts down from above.

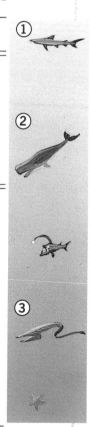

25

Little and large

I n the past 100 years, submarines have grown from tiny craft that could stay underwater for only a few hours, to great giants that can stay submerged for weeks at a time.

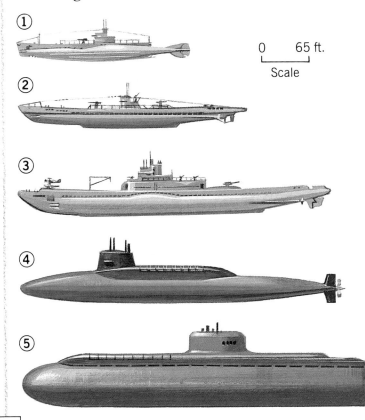

①

0   65 ft.

Scale

②

③

④

⑤

MINI-SUBS

Tiny submersibles can dive deep and do all kinds of undersea work, from exploring wrecks on the seabed to mending cables.

◁ This little robot has video cameras and arms for simple repair jobs.

▷ *Deepstar IV* can dive as deep as 4,000 feet, about four times as deep as most submarines can go.

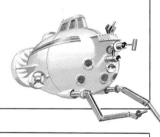

GROWING SUBMARINES

The bigger a submarine, the farther and the faster it can go.

① Most World War I submarines were small.
② German submarines are called U-boats.
③ The submarines used in World War II were bigger and there were more of them.
④ Five of these U.S. Navy submarines were launched in 1960.
⑤ At over 500 feet long, the Russian Typhoons are the world's biggest.

Future designs

In the future, smaller submarines may be made once again. They will be faster, too, making them even harder to discover. Some will be robots which can be controlled from a distance. Robot submarines can do jobs that would be too dangerous if there was a human crew on board.

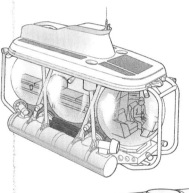

◁ Gemini is a mini-sub for tourists. Its big bubble windows give spectacular views.

▽ The Spur will be a robot that stands on the seabed, waiting to attack enemies.

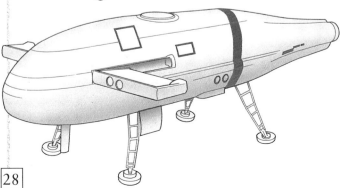

DRAWING SUBMARINES

It isn't too difficult to draw submarines. All you need to do is to start with the basic shape, then fill in the details a little at a time.

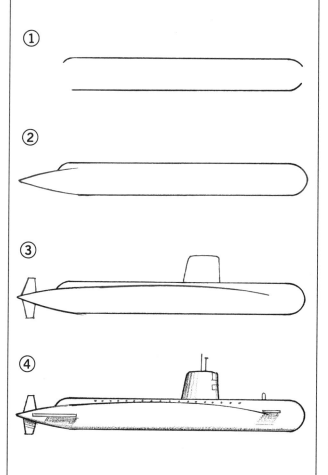

Index

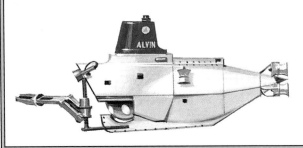